Peanuts Don't Grow On Trees!

Jeremy and Josie Schroeder

walnut

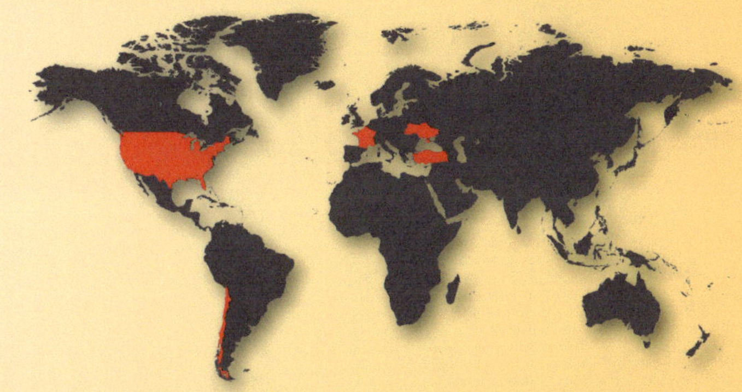

Walnuts grow
on trees.

coconut

Coconuts grow on palm trees.

cashew

Cashews grow on trees.

peanut

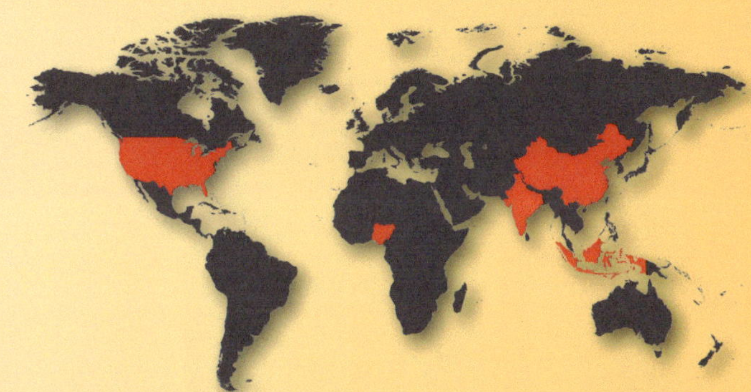

Peanuts grow
in the ground.

almond

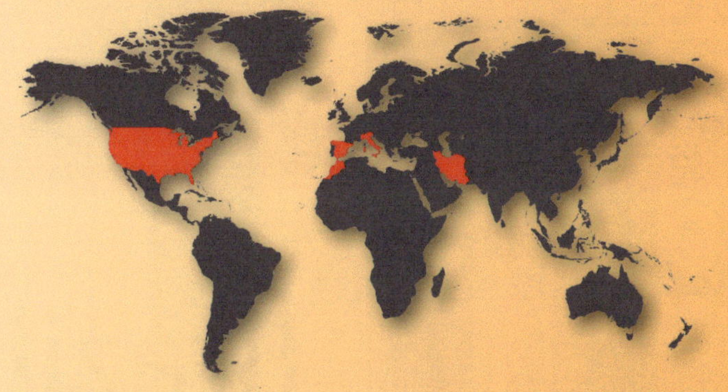

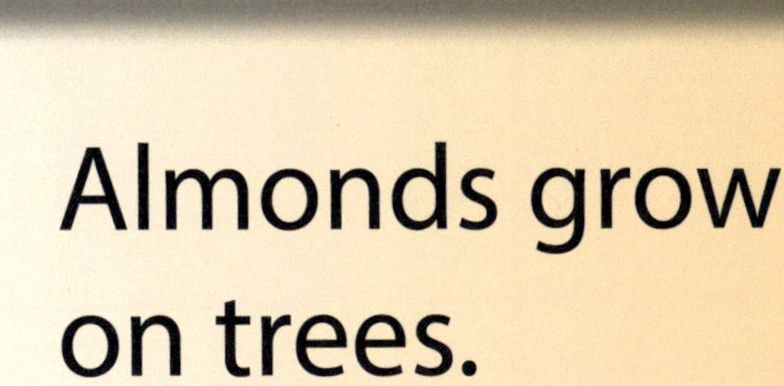

Almonds grow
on trees.

Brazil nut

Brazil nuts grow on trees.

chestnut

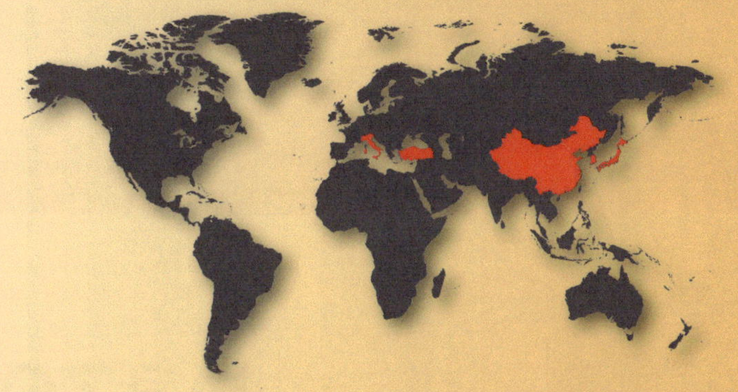

Chestnuts grow on trees.

hazelnut

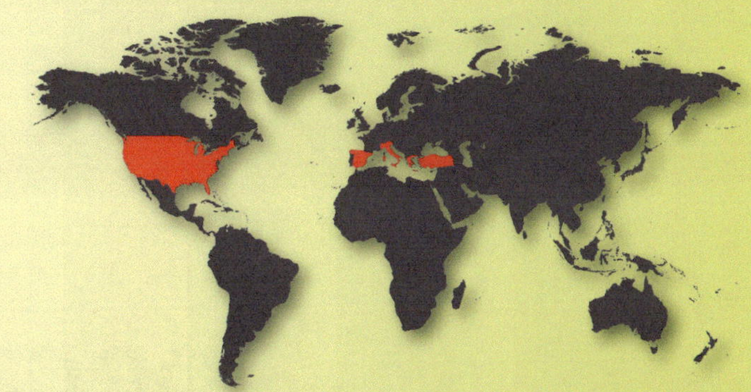

Hazelnuts grow
on trees.

pecan

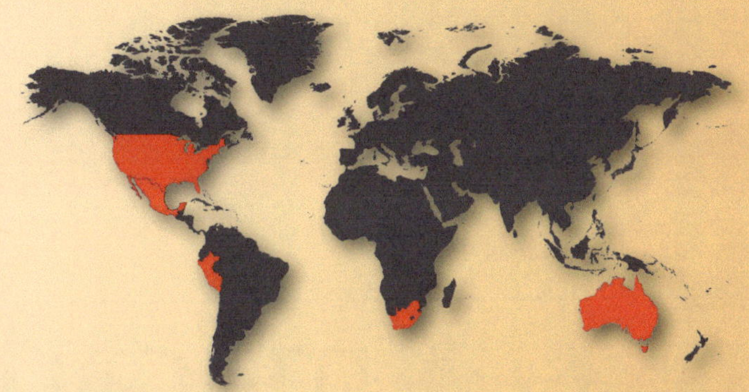

Pecans grow
on trees.

macadamia

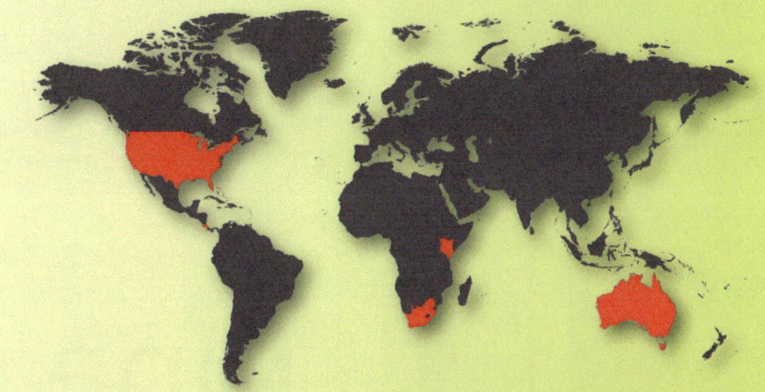

Macadamias grow on trees.

pine nut

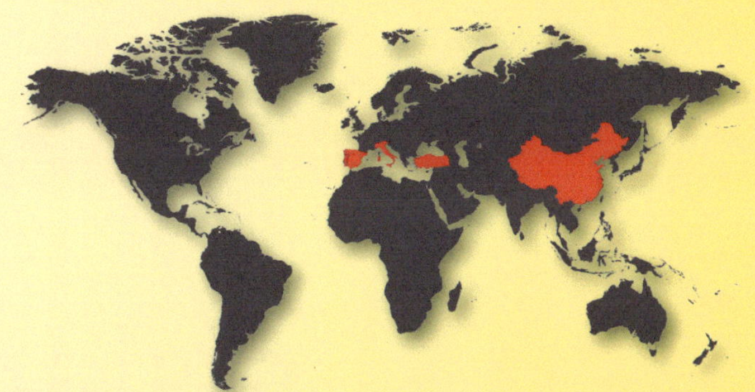

Pine nuts grow
on trees.

pistachio

Pistachios grow
on trees.

ISBN 978-91-88111-02-9

Hidden Toadstool Publishing; Linköping, Sweden; jeremy.josie.schroeder@gmail.com

Special thanks to Åsa Thor for design assistance.

Images and illustrations licensed from www.shutterstock.com

<u>Front/Back cover</u>
text- VOOK
tree- Matthew Cole
squirrel- Matthew Cole
peanut- SlipFloat
clouds- Teguh Mujiono
flower- hehehe
grass- hehehe

<u>Title page</u>
text- VOOK
tree- Matthew Cole
peanut- SlipFloat

<u>Credit spread</u>
squirrel- Matthew Cole
peanut- SlipFloat

<u>Legend for images</u>

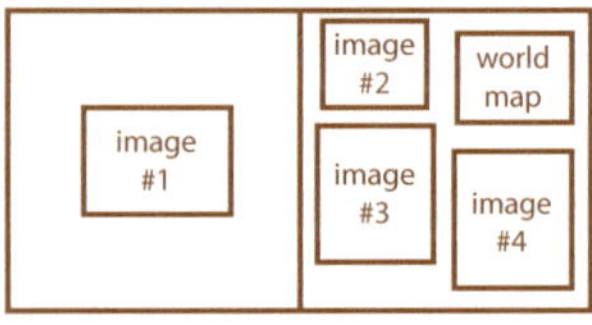

<u>World map</u>
Serban Bogdan

<u>Walnut</u>
image #1- leungchopan
image #2- Dionisvera
image #3- Olga Kovalenko
image #4- Marina Lohrbach

<u>Coconut</u>
image #1- EM Arts
image #2- Ewa Studio
image #3- Kittichai
image #4- Phiseksit

<u>Cashew</u>
image #1- Dancestrokes
image #2- Iv Nikolny
image #3- Aggie 11
image #4- Aggie 11

<u>Peanut</u>
image #1- Nikola Bilic
image #2- Sergio33
image #3- itman__47
image #4- viphotos

<u>Almond</u>
image #1- Mivr
image #2- matin
image #3- Franck Boston
image #4- nito

<u>Brazil nut</u>
image #1- Leonid Shcheglov
image #2- zcw
image #3- guentermanaus
image #4- nessa_flame

<u>Chestnut</u>
image #1- GeorgeMPhotography
image #2- Natursports
image #3- patjo
image #4- Michael Zmasser-Drexler

<u>Hazelnut</u>
image #1- Roxana Bashyrova
image #2- Valentina Razumova
image #3- Vlad Siaber
image #4- Irmantas Arnauskas

<u>Pecan</u>
image #1- Madlen
image #2- zcw
image #3- Sergio Schnitzler
image #4- Viktoriya Field

<u>Macadamia</u>
image #1- nito
image #2- JIANG HONGYAN
image #3- joloei
image #4- apiguide

<u>Pinenut</u>
image #1- m.iskandarov
image #2- Vorobyeva
image #3- Feliks Gurevich
image #4- Don Bendickson

<u>Pistachio</u>
image #1- Roxana Bashyrova
image #2- Diana Taliun
image #3- Myrmidon
image #4- Myrmidon

Made in the USA
Monee, IL
07 July 2026